Tonka

WORKING HARD WITH THE MIGHTY BACKHOE™

Written by Justine Korman
Illustrated by Steven James Petruccio

SCHOLASTIC INC.
New York   Toronto   London   Auckland   Sydney

ISBN 0-590-02378-0

TONKA® and TONKA® logo are trademarks of Hasbro, Inc.
Used with permission.
Copyright © 1998 by Hasbro, Inc. All rights reserved.
Published by Scholastic Inc.

10 9 8 7   03

Printed in the U.S.A.   23
First printing, October 1998

It's moving day! Mom tells Billy he can bring only one toy with him in the moving van. "I don't want you to lose anything," she says. Billy grabs his backhoe. Billy loves trucks, and the backhoe is his favorite!

The backhoe is the truck-of-all-trucks.
It can dig like an excavator and doze like a bulldozer.
Billy knows that dozing doesn't mean taking a nap.

To construction workers, dozing means
pushing rocks or dirt out of the way.

That's not all the backhoe can do!
The backhoe can load like a loader.
It can dump buckets full of rocks or dirt.

And, with the clamshell attached to its arm,
a backhoe can grab things, just like a crane.

Backhoes are like two trucks in one! They have controls in the back as well as the front. Some backhoe cabs have windows all around. This way the operator can see the job whether it is in front of or behind the truck.

Some backhoes even have a special chair in the middle of the cab. This chair can spin around, like the chair in Dad's office. Billy wants to have a swivel chair when he grows up.

Billy watches the driver of the moving van drive his long panel truck. The van doesn't have half the controls of a backhoe!

The moving van has the usual driving controls. There are gears that tell the van to move forward, or backward, or to stand still. More controls work the horn, lights, heat and air conditioning, turn signals, and windshield wipers. Gauges on the dashboard show how fast the van is traveling; whether it needs oil or a new battery; and if the engine is running too hot.

The driver uses his right foot to press the accelerator pedal and the brakes. And, of course, he steers with the steering wheel.

A backhoe has all of these driving controls — and more! Like most building machines, backhoes also have hydraulic controls.

Billy doesn't understand hydraulics yet. (Dad says that "hydraulics" means "liquids under pressure moving heavy things.") Billy just knows that hydraulics control the best parts of the backhoe: the front loader arm and its attachments, and the boom in the back with its dipper arm and bucket.

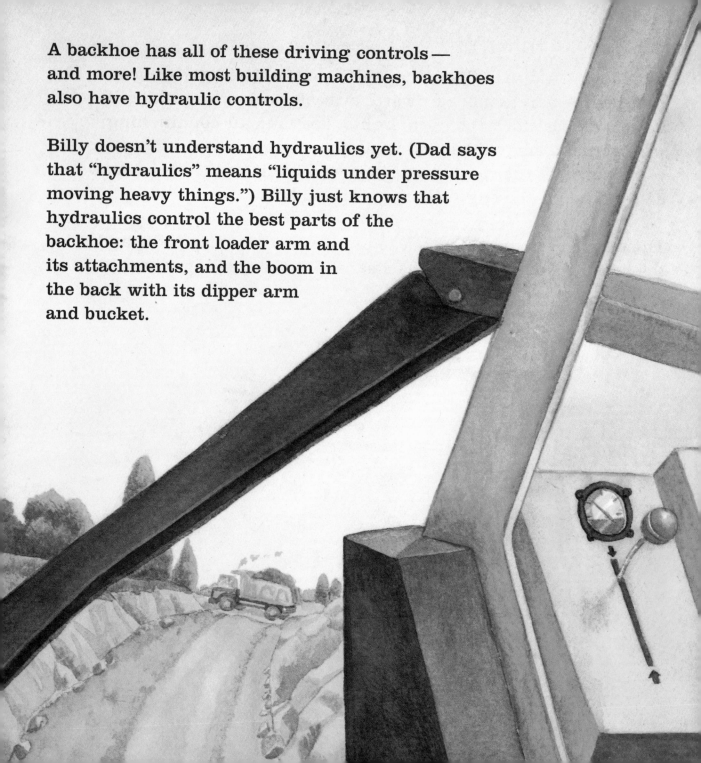

At the new house, the driver shifts the van into park, shuts off the engine, and pulls up the parking brake. Then all the adults start carrying boxes from the truck into the house. It is hard work!

Billy thinks it would be much easier with a backhoe. With the clamshell attachment, the front loader arm can lift the boxes. Then the operator can carefully swing the arm to release the box right at the front door.

Mom takes a break from moving boxes to show Billy their new garden. She points to a sunny patch of ground and says, "That is where we're going to plant the vegetable garden."

Billy looks at the lumpy ground. "A backhoe can grade that a lot faster than Dad can with a shovel," he says. Mom smiles. "Why don't you stay here and play with your truck?" she asks.

Billy plays with his backhoe for a little while.
Then he hears a boy's voice yell,
"Stand clear for blasting!"
A chorus of children shout: "KA-BOOM!"

Billy peeks over the fence and sees a group of kids
playing with trucks in a sandbox. Billy calls out,
"Can I play, too?"

The children look at Billy and his backhoe.
"We have all the trucks we need," says the biggest boy.
"Who needs a backhoe, anyway?" echoes his friend.

That is the silliest thing Billy has ever heard!
Everyone needs a backhoe! Soon, Billy imagines all the
things his busy backhoe can do.

"Today, let's help build a new road. Engage remote boom lock!"
Billy says aloud to his toy. He pretends to pull the lever that
locks the backhoe's boom in place. Billy doesn't want the boom
swinging around while his truck is on the highway.

At the work site, Billy pulls another lever.
"Engage stabilizer jacks!" he shouts. Hydraulic controls push out two sturdy metal legs. The stabilizer jacks hold the backhoe steady during heavy work. They also take the weight off the truck's wheels and tires.

Billy surveys the site. "First we have to break up the big rocks," he tells his truck. "We'll use the hydraulic hammer!"
The backhoe's hammer is much bigger and stronger than any hammer a man can hold. It makes short work of the rocks.

"Now it's time to move dirt!" Billy exclaims.
"We'll use the front arm shovel."
Billy pretends to be both the foreman
and the backhoe operator.
He shouts orders to himself.

Billy pretends to work the hydraulic controls
to move the arm exactly where he wants and
to hold the shovel at just the right angle.

Billy is so busy with his backhoe, he doesn't realize he is being watched. The children from the sandbox see Billy pretending to build the new road.

Suddenly Billy hears a boy say,
"The new kid really knows his trucks!"

Billy turns around and recognizes the biggest boy.
He smiles, and the boy smiles back.
"I'm Nick. I guess you can play with us now," the big boy offers.
Soon Billy's backhoe is busy helping to build a skyscraper in
Nick's sandbox.

But that's no surprise. Billy knew all along:
Everyone needs a backhoe!